SNOW WHITE
AND THE
SEVEN DWARFS

A PARRAGON BOOK

Published by
Parragon Books,
Unit 13–17, Avonbridge Trading Estate,
Atlantic Road, Avonmouth, Bristol BS11 9QD.

Produced by
The Templar Company plc,
Pippbrook Mill, London Road, Dorking, Surrey RH4 1JE.

Copyright © 1994 Parragon Book Service Limited

Designed by Mark Kingsley-Monks

Printed and bound in Great Britain

ISBN 1-85813-685-7

MINI CLASSICS

SNOW WHITE
AND THE
SEVEN DWARFS

RETOLD BY STEPHANIE LASLETT
ILLUSTRATED BY BRIAN ROBERTSON

Once upon a time, in the middle of winter when the snowflakes were falling like feathers on the ground, a Queen sat by her black ebony windowsill and sewed. She was watching the snow form a white blanket over the ground when she suddenly pricked her finger.

Three drops of blood fell upon the snow outside and the Queen stared at them, lost in thought. She looked at the white, the red, and the black and she softly sighed to herself.

"Oh! what wouldn't I give to have a child as white as snow, as red as blood, and as black as ebony!"

In time her wish was granted, for not long after this, a little daughter was born to her. She had skin as white as snow, lips and cheeks as red as blood, and hair as black as ebony, and they called her Snow White. But sad to say, not long after her birth the Queen grew ill and died.

After a year the King married again. His new wife was a very beautiful woman, but so proud and haughty that she could not bear to think anyone was more lovely than she.

She possessed a magic mirror, and every day she would gaze at her own reflection and ask:

"Mirror, mirror, on the wall,
Who has the fairest
face of all?"
And the mirror would reply:
"You are most fair,
my Lady Queen,
No fairer face was ever seen."
Then the Queen was
happy for she knew her
magic mirror always spoke
the truth.

But as the years went by, little Snow White grew prettier and prettier every day, and she was as good as she was pretty.

Time passed and by the time she was seventeen years old she was more beautiful than any girl ever seen, and fairer even than the Queen herself.

One day when the Queen
asked her mirror the usual
question, it replied:
"My Lady Queen,
you are fair, 'tis true,
But Snow White is fairer
far than you."

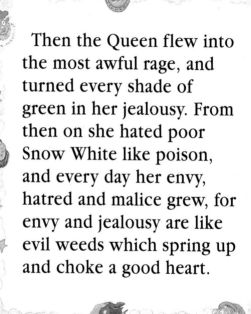

Then the Queen flew into the most awful rage, and turned every shade of green in her jealousy. From then on she hated poor Snow White like poison, and every day her envy, hatred and malice grew, for envy and jealousy are like evil weeds which spring up and choke a good heart.

At last the Queen resolved to get rid of Snow White forever and calling a huntsman to her, she said:

"Take the child out into the wood and never let me see her face again. You must kill her and bring me back her heart and liver, so I may know for certain that she is dead."

The Huntsman did as he was told and led Snow White deep into the wood, but as he was about to draw his knife and kill her, she began to cry.

"Oh, dear Huntsman, spare my life, and I will promise to run far away into the wood and never return home again."

And because she was so young and innocent, the Huntsman took pity on her and let her go.

As she ran off into the dark forest he wondered whether she would be safe, for he feared the wild beasts might find her. But his heart felt lighter because he hadn't had to

do the evil deed himself.
  On his way back to the
castle he shot a young boar
and brought its heart and
liver home to the Queen as
proof that Snow White was
indeed dead. And then the
wicked woman was well
pleased and congratulated
herself on getting rid of
Snow White for ever.

Now when the poor child
found herself alone in the
big wood she grew afraid.
The trees seemed to form
strange shapes, and she felt
so frightened she didn't
know what to do. Then
she began to run over the
sharp stones, and through
bramble bushes, and the
wild beasts watched her go.

She ran as far as her legs would carry her, and as evening approached she feared she could go no further. Then, to her joy, she saw a little house in a clearing and she stumbled up the path to the door.

Everything inside was very small but as clean and as nice as a bright new pin.

In the middle of the room there stood a wooden table covered with a white cloth. It was laid with seven little plates and forks and spoons and knives and mugs. Side by side against the wall there were seven little beds covered with bright patchwork quilts.

Snow White felt so hungry

and so thirsty that she ate a
bit of bread and a little
porridge from each plate,
and drank a drop of wine
out of each cup. Then,
feeling tired and sleepy,
she lay down on one of the
beds, but it was hard and
lumpy and not at all
comfortable. So she tried
all the others in turn.

But one was too long, and another too short, and it was only when she got to the seventh that she found one to suit her exactly. So she lay down upon it, said her prayers like a good child, and fell fast asleep.

When it got quite dark the masters of the little house returned.

They were seven Dwarfs and all day long they worked in the mines, right down deep in the heart of the mountains.

Stepping inside the door, they lit their seven little lamps, and as soon as their eyes grew accustomed to the glare they saw that someone had been in the

room. Holding their lamps
high, they looked all around.
Then the first Dwarf
noticed that his chair had
been moved from its place.

"Who's been sitting on
my little chair?" he asked.

"Who's been eating my
little loaf?" said the second.

"Who's been tasting my
porridge?" added the third.

"Who's been eating out of my little plate?" said the fourth Dwarf, with a frown. "And who's been using my little fork?" said the fifth.

The sixth held up his mug and scowled.

"And who's been drinking out of my little mug?" he demanded.

Then the first Dwarf turned round and saw a little hollow in his bed.

"Who's been lying on my bed?" he asked.

The others came running and when they saw that their beds, too, were crumpled they cried:

"Somebody has been lying on our beds as well."

But when the seventh Dwarf looked at his bed, he stepped back in surprise, for there was Snow White fast asleep. Then he called to the others and when they saw Snow White lying there they could hardly believe their eyes.

"Goodness gracious!"

they cried together. "What a beautiful child!"

And they were so enchanted by her sweet innocence that they did not wake her, but let her sleep on in the little bed. The seventh Dwarf slept for one hour at a time in each of his companions' beds, and so the night passed by.

In the morning Snow White awoke, rested and refreshed, but when she saw the seven little Dwarfs gathered around her bed she was afraid. The little men were so friendly and asked her what her name was in such a kind way, that at last she replied: "I am Snow White."

39

"Why did you come here?"
asked the inquisitive
Dwarfs. Then Snow White
told them her sad story
and they were very
shocked by her wicked
stepmother's evil plan.

"Will you stay and keep
house for us?" asked the
first Dwarf. "Here you will
be quite safe from harm."

"You could cook and make the beds," continued the second Dwarf.

"And do the washing and the mending," added the third, nodding his head. "Can you sew? Can you knit?" piped up the fourth.

"Oh, do say you'll stay!" they all begged together. "You will be happy with us."

"Yes!" laughed Snow White. "I will gladly stay with you here."

And so it was. Every morning the Dwarfs went into the mountains to dig for gold, and in the evening, when they returned home, Snow White always had their supper ready for them.

But during the day the girl was left quite alone and the good Dwarfs worried about her safety. Each day as they left they warned her to take care.

"Beware of your stepmother. She will soon find out that you are here, so whatever you do, don't let anyone into the house."

Meanwhile, back at the castle the Queen was happy in the belief that she was once more the most beautiful woman in all the land. But one day she went to her mirror and asked:
"Mirror, mirror,
on the wall,
Who has the fairest
face of all?"

The proud woman smiled
at her reflection and waited
for the mirror's reply:
"My Lady Queen,
you are fair, 'tis true,
But Snow White is fairer
far than you.
Snow White, who dwells
with the seven small men,
Is as fair as you,
and as fair again."

When the Queen heard these words she was nearly struck dumb with horror, for the mirror always spoke the truth. Now she knew that the Huntsman must have deceived her, and that Snow White was still alive. She pondered day and night how she might destroy her rival.

Her jealous heart gave her no peace until at last she thought of a plan. She disguised herself as an old tinker woman in a shabby bonnet and shawl. She leaned upon a crooked stick and carried a large basket upon her bent back. No-one would ever guess she was the evil Queen.

And so she set off to hobble over the seven hills until she came to the house of the seven Dwarfs. There she knocked at the door and called out:

"Fine wares to sell, fine wares to sell!"

Timidly, Snow White peeped out of the window and smiled at the old crone.

"Good-day to you, and what have you to sell?"

"Good wares, fine wares," the old woman answered. "Laces of every shade and description," and she held up a long length of brightly coloured silk.

"This honest old woman is certainly not my evil stepmother. Surely I can let her in," thought Snow White, so she unbarred the door and bought some laces.

"Come, child," said the old woman. "Your bodice is coming undone. Let me lace you up properly for once and make you tidy."

And so Snow White, suspecting no evil, let the old woman enter the house.

But the old woman laced her so quickly and so tightly that she squeezed all the air from her body. Snow White could not draw another breath and fell lifeless to the floor.

"Now you are no longer the fairest," laughed the wicked old woman, and then she hurried away.

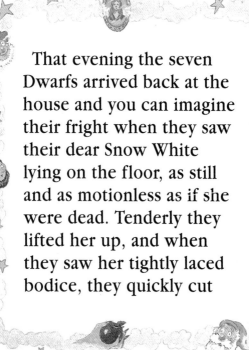

That evening the seven Dwarfs arrived back at the house and you can imagine their fright when they saw their dear Snow White lying on the floor, as still and as motionless as if she were dead. Tenderly they lifted her up, and when they saw her tightly laced bodice, they quickly cut the lace in two. Then Snow White began to breathe a little and gradually came back to life.

"That old tinker woman was the evil Queen," said the Dwarves, when they heard what had happened.

"From now on you must be extra careful and be sure to let no-one in at all."

Back at the castle the
Queen had gone straight to
her mirror as soon as she
reached home and said:
"Mirror, mirror,
on the wall,
Who has the fairest
face of all?"
Her eyes glittered as she
waited to hear the magic
mirror's reply.

"My Lady Queen,
you are fair, 'tis true,
But Snow White is fairer
far than you.
Snow White, who dwells
with the seven small men,
Is as fair as you,
and as fair again."
When the Queen heard
these words she trembled
and shook with rage.

"Snow White shall die,"
she cried. "I will even risk
my own life to make sure
she meets her end."

Then she went to a secret
little room which no-one
knew of but herself, and
there she carefully made a
poisoned apple. It certainly
looked beautiful, with one
white cheek and one red.

Anyone who saw it would
long to eat it, but if they
did so they would certainly
die on the spot. When the
apple was quite finished
the wicked Queen disguised
herself as an old peasant
and set off over the seven
hills to the house of the
seven Dwarfs. This time
her plan would not fail!

Once again, she knocked at the door and invited Snow White to taste her beautiful apple.

"I must not let anyone in," replied Snow White. "The seven Dwarfs have forbidden me to do so."

"Are you afraid of being poisoned?" asked the old woman. "See, I will cut the apple in half. I will eat the white cheek and you can eat the red."

But the apple was so

cleverly made that only the red cheek was poisonous.

Snow White longed to eat the tempting fruit, and when she saw that the old peasant woman was eating it herself, she could resist no longer. She stretched out her hand for the poisonous half and took a small bite.

But hardly had it passed her lips than she fell down dead upon the ground. Then the eyes of the cruel Queen sparkled with glee as she cried:

"As white as snow, as red as blood and as black as ebony you are, but this time the Dwarfs will not bring you back to life."

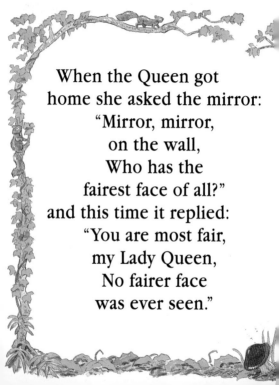

When the Queen got
home she asked the mirror:
"Mirror, mirror,
on the wall,
Who has the
fairest face of all?"
and this time it replied:
"You are most fair,
my Lady Queen,
No fairer face
was ever seen."

Then her jealous heart was at rest — at least, as much at rest as a jealous heart can ever be.

When the little Dwarfs came home in the evening they found Snow White lying on the ground, and she neither breathed nor stirred. Silent with misery, they laid her upon a bed.

Then they searched the house for clues to explain what might have happened but nothing was found. They unlaced her bodice, combed her hair, washed her face, but all in vain. The child was dead and remained dead.

Tenderly they placed her on a bier, and then all the seven Dwarfs sat round it, sobbing and weeping for three whole days. At last they decided they would have to bury her, but she looked so beautiful and fresh and her cheeks glowed so pink that they could not bring themselves to do it.

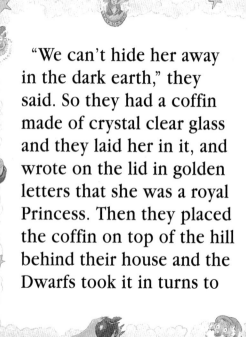

"We can't hide her away in the dark earth," they said. So they had a coffin made of crystal clear glass and they laid her in it, and wrote on the lid in golden letters that she was a royal Princess. Then they placed the coffin on top of the hill behind their house and the Dwarfs took it in turns to stay and keep watch over her. And soon the birds came and silently mourned Snow White's death — first an owl, and then a raven, and last of all a little dove.

As the days passed, there were no changes to be seen in Snow White. She always looked just as if she were in a deep, deep sleep.

There she lay with her skin as white as snow, her lips as red as blood, and her hair as black as ebony.

Now it happened one day that a Prince came to the wood and, looking up, he saw the coffin on the hill. There he found the beautiful Snow White and he fell in love at first sight. When he had read what was written in golden letters, he said to the Dwarf sitting close by:

"Please sell me this glass coffin and I'll pay whatever price you ask."

But the Dwarf shook his head. "We would not part with it for all the gold in the world," he said.

"Then make me a gift of this treasure," begged the Prince," and I will cherish it as my dearest possession."

He spoke so sadly that the good Dwarfs had pity on him and gave him the coffin, and the Prince made his servants carry it away on their shoulders.

But as they were going down the hill they stumbled over a bush, and jolted the coffin so violently that the poisonous bit of apple fell out of Snow White's throat.

Then she slowly opened her eyes, lifted up the lid of the coffin, and to the Prince's great delight, sat up alive and well.

"What has happened?"
she cried. "Where am I?"
Joyfully, the Prince
explained. "Now you are
safe with me," he said and
he told her all that had
happened, adding, "I love
you better than anyone in
the whole wide world. Will
you come with me to my
palace and be my wife?"

The Dwarfs clapped and cheered as Snow White happily agreed and the marriage was arranged to take place a few days later.

Now the wicked Queen was invited to the Prince's wedding feast but she did not know the name of the bride. As soon as she was dressed in all her finery,

she went to the mirror and
said haughtily:
       "Mirror, mirror,
         on the wall,
       Who has the fairest
         face of all?"
Then the mirror answered:
       "My Lady Queen,
       you are fair, 'tis true,
       But the Prince's new bride
         is fairer than you."

When the wicked woman heard these words she flew into a terrible rage and hurried to the feast to face her rival.

When she saw that it was Snow White her anger was so terrible that it gripped her heart and, with a terrible scream, she fell down dead.

And so Snow White and the Prince were married in great splendour with a ring of gold lovingly crafted by the seven clever Dwarves. And, as with all good fairy tales, they all lived happily ever after.

JACOB AND WILHELM GRIMM

The German Brothers Grimm, Jacob (1785-1863) and Wilhelm (1786-1859) gathered together over 200 old folk tales to form the classic collection of stories now known as *Grimm's Fairy Tales*.

Before this time, *Snow White and the Seven Dwarfs* and the other tales would have been part of an oral tradition of storytelling. Retold from generation to generation, they passed on important truths about everyday life and our fellow creatures: good would be rewarded and evil would not go unpunished. A child's hidden anxieties were given shape in the form of witches and ogres and they saw that time and again, the underdog would emerge victor.

These simple messages remain a valuable contribution to each child's development of a sense of "right" and "wrong" and help explain why *Grimm's Fairy Tales* are so well-loved throughout the world.